Max Greebly

and the

MYSTERY OF THE

Bawling Bank Robbers

Dave Hammer

MAX GREEBLY AND THE MYSTERY OF THE
BAWLING BANK ROBBERS
Copyright © 2014 by Dave Hammer

This is a work of fiction. Names, characters, places and incidents either
are the product of the author's imagination or are used fictitiously,
and any resemblance to actual persons, living or dead, businesses,
companies, events, or locales is entirely coincidental.

Printed in Canada

ISBN: 978-1-4866-0138-7

Word Alive Press
131 Cordite Road, Winnipeg, MB R3W 1S1
www.wordalivepress.ca

MIX
Paper from
responsible sources
FSC® C016245

Library and Archives Canada Cataloguing in Publication

Hammer, Dave, 1967-, author
    Max Greebly and the mystery of the bawling bank robbers
/ Dave Hammer.

ISBN 978-1-4866-0138-7 (pbk.)

    I. Title.

PS8615.A462M39 2013   jC813'.6   C2013-905247-X

To my nephew, James.

CHAPTER 1

CYRUS THE HEDGEHOG HEARD BUZZING AS HE RAN lightly though the grass. His young master, Max Greebly, must be up shaving already, Cyrus thought. As he turned the corner of the neighbor's house, Cyrus nearly ran into a lawnmower. The buzzing of its blade sounded much louder now that he was face to face with it. Oops, guess it wasn't his master shaving after all. Come to think of it, Cyrus had never seen Max shave. He cut around the mower as the neighbor pushed it mindlessly around the yard. The neighbor never saw him.

When Cyrus got into his house, he ran upstairs to the room he shared with Max. The door was slightly open so he slipped in to find Max stuffing all the pockets of his cargo pants. A bunch of marbles, mini flashlight, and some candy found their way in.

Max had gotten the marbles for Christmas, even though he had wanted a cell phone. His dad thought he was too young for a cell.

"I played with them when I was your age," his dad had said.

"But no one plays with them anymore!" Max complained.

His dad explained that you could use marbles for many different things, so Max was going to take just a quarter of the marbles with him to see if he could find a fun use for them.

He'd just slipped his favorite pocketknife into his pocket and zipped it shut when he saw Cyrus standing on his hind legs watching him.

"Come on, Cyrus, let's go on an adventure!"

Eleven-year-old Max bounded out of the room, down the stairs, and out the front door with Cyrus running right behind him. First they went to the park and hid among the trees, spying on the people at the playground. They saw the kids using the slide, teeter-totter, and swings while parents watched. Some parents were even taking care of little babies while watching the older children play.

After spying for a while, they moved on to the ice cream shop, where Max debated about whether to get the cookie dough, cotton candy, or bubble gum flavor. He finally settled on a double-scoop of cotton candy, and used a little of his allowance to pay. He even let Cyrus have a few licks as they lay on the grass next door.

After eating, they wandered around town. When Cyrus got tired, Max put him in his shirt pocket, where Cyrus' little head poked out as he watched with interest everything around them.

After a long day of playing, Max headed back home. They were just past the bank when they heard a loud bang. Max turned to see a man run out of the bank holding a large bag, stuffed full, with a gun in his hand.

"It's a bank robber, Cyrus," Max whispered, crouching down so Cyrus could jump out of his pocket. As he watched the bank robber, Max got an idea for those marbles. He whipped the bag out of his cargo pocket, gave a handful to Cyrus, took a handful for himself, and bowled the marbles down the sidewalk towards the robber.

A second man, also holding a large bag and a gun, ran out of the bank. He stepped on one of Max's marbles and yelped as his feet flew up. Down on the ground he went, crying like a baby.

A third man rushed out of the bank. Seeing his fallen friend, he turned to the right, directly towards Max and Cyrus. Cyrus sucked a bunch of marbles in his mouth, then started shooting them in rapid fire. Fffut, fffut, fffut, fffut, fffut. The man running towards them slipped on one and lost his balance, crashing to the ground, moaning.

3

The first bank robber, who had just stood there the whole time while the marbles all rolled by him, suddenly took off, leaping over the second man who still lay on the ground. Max grabbed the bag of marbles and sent the rest of them rolling toward the first bank robber. The marbles spread out as they rolled.

Cyrus started shooting his rapid-fire marbles again, and the robber got only a few steps past his fallen friend when his feet shot up straight in the air as he fell.

Then Max heard sirens. A minute later, the police were putting the three men into the backs of several police cars, all the while slipping and sliding on the marbles scattered all over the ground. A large crowd had formed to watch the action. When they finally got the three robbers in the backs of three police cars, one police officer walked over to Max and Cyrus.

"Hello, son. I'm Detective Mallory. Are those your marbles all over the street?"

"Yes sir, they are."

"Well, you did a fine job slowing those bank robbers down until we got here."

"Do you think I could get my marbles back?"

"That shouldn't be too difficult. Do you know how many you had?"

"Fifty, sir!" Max said proudly.

The officer patted Max on the head. "Just wait here and I'll see what I can do." He walked back to where the other officers stood surrounded by the crowd. Max noticed the squad cars had left with the bank robbers. Detective Mallory talked to one of the other officers at the scene for a moment, then the officer handed Mallory a megaphone.

"Ladies and gentlemen, that young boy over there," he said, pointing to Max, "stopped the bank robbers who were about to make off with hundreds of thousands of dollars. He did it all with his marbles, which you'll see all over the street. Would you be so kind as to help us collect all fifty and return them to their owner?"

The crowd cheered for Max, and he turned bright red. Then they started picking up his marbles. Before long, Max had all fifty secured back in his marble bag.

The police officer drove Max and Cyrus home and told Max's parents and his sister Tara what he had done. Mr. Greebly beamed with pride as the officer recapped the afternoon events down at the bank.

CHAPTER 2

DURING SUPPER, MAX RECOUNTED THE DAY'S GREAT adventure.

"You should have seen us, Mom! We took out those robbers with just a bag of marbles!" His face was all lit up as he grinned at his mom, dad and sister Tara. "Cyrus and I should fight crime all the time!"

"Maybe there's a crime reported in the newspaper that you and Cyrus could solve. Like junior detectives," his dad said.

"I'm not a junior detective, Dad! I'm almost twelve!"

Feeling foolish, Max's dad said, "You're right, son. You won't be like a junior detective, but a real detective. Just let your mom and I know what you're up to at all times. Maybe we can help you in some way."

"Yeah right, Dad!" Max said, driving his fork deep into his potatoes and taking a big bite.

After supper, Mrs. Greebly started putting the food away and clearing the dishes and putting them into the dishwasher.

"Max, I want you to clean Cyrus' cage tonight. It hasn't been cleaned in a while and it stinks. It's starting to smell up the whole house!"

"But Mom! Tara's in the bathroom taking a shower, so I can't put Cyrus in the tub while I clean his cage. She takes forever in there!"

"Stop complaining and just go clean it. You can leave Cyrus in the cage while you do it."

Max slowly climbed the stairs and went into his bedroom. "Why can't you clean your own cage?" he asked, looking at his hedgehog pal.

Cyrus just stared at Max. So Max tried to clean around Cyrus. Cyrus didn't like it. He kept charging Max's hand, jumping at him with his head quills, sticking them out like a battering ram. You see, hedgehogs have sharp quills on their back and head that they can raise up to protect themselves. When hedgehogs are not angry or upset, the quills lie flat on their body and head.

Thankfully, Max was quick. He pulled his hand away each time Cyrus jumped at him. Max was almost finished cleaning the cage when Cyrus finally got him, poking his hand with those quills. "Owww!" Max hollered. "Mom! Cyrus stabbed me in the hand with his quills!"

"Just put a bandage on it, dear," Mrs. Greebly called from the kitchen.

Max glared at Cyrus and Cyrus glared right back, his head pushed forward aggressively and all his quills standing up. He looked so mad, Max shrugged and went back downstairs where he found a bandage and put it over the pinholes in his hand.

That night, Max was sleeping peacefully in his bed on the second floor when a noise woke him up. Then he heard it again. It sounded like someone was walking on the floor downstairs. He heard a crunching sound as if the floor were covered in potato chips or eggshells. Maybe it was a burglar!

He lay there in bed trying to figure it out. It made no sense. Why would a burglar spread chips or eggshells on the floor and then be forgetful enough to walk on them? Max decided he'd better go look. As he got up, he looked over at Cyrus' cage. Cyrus was standing on his hind legs with his front feet against the bars of his cage and looking eager to help catch the prowler.

Slipping Cyrus into his pajama shirt pocket, Max picked up his bat from the floor. Then he sneaked out of his room and down the hall, tiptoeing his way across the carpet. Slowly, cautiously, he crept down the stairs. Down at the bottom he walked on cat feet through the large foyer, then the dining room, until he could see the kitchen beyond, hidden in darkness. That's where the crunching sounds were coming from. *That must be one dumb burglar*, he thought.

He could feel Cyrus stirring in his pocket and knew he wanted out. Max picked him up and set him gingerly on the floor. "Attack!" he whispered.

Cyrus took off, his little toe nails clicking softly on the tile as he tore across the kitchen. A second later, Max heard a howl from the thief.

Max snapped on the light and caught the trespasser in the bright lights. There stood a barefoot man in his pajamas looking shocked. There was a bowl of granola on the counter in front of him. Max saw a red spot on the man's bare big toe and knew that Cyrus had pricked him with his quills. There was no sign of Cyrus. He had probably figured out who the intruder was just after stabbing him with his quills and run away before he was seen.

"Dad! Why are you eating cereal in the dark?"

CHAPTER 3

IN THE MORNING, EVERYONE WAS TALKING AT ONCE.

"Cyrus poked Dad with his quills last night! We thought he was a burglar!"

"Honey, you're looking a little tired this morning. Did you have trouble sleeping last night?"

"Are the eggs done yet?"

Eventually breakfast was eaten, the dishes were all put in the dishwasher, and the kitchen was empty again. Max got a book and sat down on the living room sofa while his dad read the newspaper beside him.

"Here you go, Max," Mr. Greebly said. "It says here that five banks in the area have been robbed, and the police think this is part of a large gang. In fact, they say despite catching three robbers, thanks to you, there is more of this gang out there. Now if you could figure out what bank they're going to rob next, you could see what the robbers look like and tell the police. But you be careful—don't let them see you or you might be in danger."

Spider was big and tall. His shoulders were as wide as a truck and his muscles stretched his T-shirt so tight it looked as if it might rip any second. With his short hair, thick neck, and permanent scowl, he made even the toughest guys think twice about making him mad.

"Listen boys, three of our guys got nabbed on the last bank robbery, so that only leaves eight of us now. You make sure you keep the next jobs quiet. I don't want to hear a peep about them and if the police catch you, you don't know nothin'! You got it?"

He was in a dark room, in a darker building. One light bulb tried hard to cast some light into the room, but it only lit up a table in the middle of the room. Four guys could dimly be seen in the shadows of the room. Three were Spider's closest henchmen.

The next day, Max and Cyrus went to the mall to look around. Max wanted to find a skateboard on sale. He loved skateboards and dreamed that one day soon he could afford one. Right then, he was hoping he'd find a 90%-off sale. Then a hundred-dollar skateboard would be only ten bucks. An even better sale than that, Max was thinking, would be a 110%-off sale. Then a hundred-dollar skateboard wouldn't cost him a cent. In fact, the store would pay him just for taking it home.

Max was in the large department store looking through the aisles with Cyrus in his shirt pocket when they saw an older boy stuff something in his pocket. Without making it look as if they were spying on the boy, Max kept browsing but followed the thief. Soon they saw him stuffing Kinder Surprises—foil-wrapped chocolate eggs with a small toy inside—right off the shelf into his pocket! Then he looked around guiltily and headed for the exit.

Cyrus started trying to crawl out of Max's pocket. His little legs were going a mile a minute.

"You want to get that boy, Cyrus?"

Cyrus fought even harder to get out.

Max picked him up and set him on the floor. "Go for it, boy!"

Cyrus took off like a shot. Max watched as Cyrus caught up to the boy before he left the store. Then, to Max's shock, Cyrus disappeared up inside the boy's pant leg.

A couple of seconds later, Max could see the outline of Cyrus running up the boy's leg. The boy started to twitch. Then he began a strange dance, lifting his one leg high in the air and shaking it while slowly twirling.

As Cyrus ran up the boy's pant leg, he puffed out his quills. When his quills poked the boy for the first time, he started to jump around, causing Cyrus' quills to poke him even more.

"Eeeeeeeek!" the boy screamed. "There's a mouse crawling up my pants!"

Soon several store staff were standing around watching him swing his arms round and round, and kick his leg high in the air and shake it as if he had a bee in his shoe.

Cyrus clung to the boy's pants and had the ride of his life. *Whee*, he thought, *this is better than the rides at the fair!*

Eventually the boy spun too quickly in his wild dance and he fell over. The staff all looked down and saw two Kinder Surprises roll out of his pocket onto the floor. In the distraction, Cyrus made his escape.

Mixed among the staff at the store were a couple men who worked store security. When they saw the Kinder Surprises roll out of the boy's pocket, they grabbed him and hauled him off to a back room.

Max was amazed at what Cyrus had accomplished. He stood staring for a few moments until he felt Cyrus jumping up and down on his shoe. He picked Cyrus up and was just putting him back in his pocket when one of the security guards came out from the back of the store.

"Nice pet you have there," he said.

"Thanks! His name is Cyrus."

"I saw him just after the boy fell down. He's quite a hero."

"Well, thank you, sir."

Just then, the store manager came over. "You and your pet saved us today. It wasn't expensive stuff that boy stole, but we believe he steals from us quite a bit, so we are very thankful you helped us catch him."

"Why didn't you just search him every time he left the store?" Max asked.

"We did search him a couple times. But those times he had nothing on him and when his parents threatened to sue us, we didn't dare search him unless we knew for sure he had stolen something. We didn't have any proof until today. With the help of your little pet, he won't be allowed in this store anymore."

The store manager cleared his throat. "On behalf of the store, we would like to give you a fifty-dollar gift card for anything you like in our store."

Max took the gift card as if it were gold. With the money he had saved at home, he might be able to buy that skateboard after all.

"Thank you so much, sir!" Max said, looking at the manager with tears in his eyes.

The kindly manager put a warm hand on Max's shoulder. "You deserve it, son. You should be proud that you raised such a fine pet! Make sure you get something special for him, too."

Cyrus wriggled in Max's pocket. Max knew exactly what Cyrus wanted.

CHAPTER 4

THAT NIGHT AFTER SUPPER, MR. GREEBLY WASHED A bunch of strawberries that Max had bought for Cyrus. Once the stems were removed, Max took a couple up to his room to give to Cyrus. When Cyrus smelled the strawberries, he went nuts. He threw himself against his cage and rattled the bars of the door. He shook the door so hard Max thought it might pop open, but he opened it up before that happened and tossed them in. Cyrus turned, saw where the strawberries landed, then leaped high into the air. He landed right on top of one of the strawberries and attacked it with his teeth. Bits of strawberry flew in all directions as he ate it.

It was nice to see Bella after her long family vacation. Max had first met Bella at school. One day in class, she had been sitting behind him when she leaned forward and whispered in his ear, "You smell like pancakes."

Max had immediately wanted to hide in his desk. He had really hoped the pancake smell from breakfast would disappear before lunch so no one else would notice.

"I like pancakes," Bella had whispered again.

The two of them had become good friends after that.

Bella lived on the same block as Max. When he saw one morning that she was back from vacation and playing in her front yard, he ran down to see her.

"Hi!" he said.

"Hey, Max. Do you want to play?"

They played the morning away. They played catch with a beach ball and laughed when it slipped between their arms and bopped them gently on the nose.

When they were tired, Bella asked Max about his summer. He explained the two crimes he and Cyrus had stopped.

"Your dad really told you that you could figure out where the next bank robbery would be?"

"He said I might be able to if I could find a pattern. But how can I do that?"

"We could ask my mom. She likes to read those kinds of stories."

They ran into Bella's house, and found her

mom chopping vegetables in the kitchen.

"Whatcha doing, Mom?" Bella asked.

"Making soup for lunch."

"Do you remember that bank robbery a week ago, where the bank robbers got caught thanks to Max and Cyrus?"

Bella's mom looked at the two of them curiously. "What are you two up to?"

Max explained his dad's idea that he try to figure out where the next robbery would be and then only watch from a safe distance in order to identify the robbers and tell the police.

"Well if it's okay with Max's dad, I guess it's okay with me. But you be very careful or you'll be in serious trouble. Do you understand?"

"Yes, Mom."

"There have been at least three or four other bank robberies that may have been by the same gang," Bella's mom said. "The robberies only started this summer, so they shouldn't be hard for you to find in the newspaper."

"Do you still have those newspapers?" Bella asked.

"No, dear. I put them out to recycle last night, and they've been picked up already. But the library will have copies."

Max and Bella headed off to the library after lunch, and started looking through newspapers.

It wasn't long before Bella found an article about a bank robbery in town.

Then they both read the newspapers without seeing anything for a while.

"I found one!" Max shouted, forgetting where he was for a moment.

"SHHHHH," said the other people in the library.

"Oops," Max whispered, then showed what he had found to Bella.

They were through most of the newspapers by then, but kept looking in case there had been more bank robberies. Right near the bottom of the stack, they found one more story. Then they used some of their money to photocopy those stories and took their hard-earned prizes home.

When they got to Max's house, they spread the papers on the floor of the rec room and began reading. "It says here that the leader of this gang is a man known only as Spider," Bella said.

"Where's the spider!" Tara shrieked. She had just come down to the rec room.

"There's no spider. It's the name of a man," Max told her.

"Nasty name," Tara replied.

"What are you doing down here?" Max asked.

"I just came to get a movie and then I'm going back to my room to watch it on my computer!"

After Tara left, they finished reading the articles. Max got a map of the city from his parents. Then he and Bella tacked it up on the wall in the rec room. They used colored pins to mark where the robberies had taken place, including the one Max and Cyrus stopped. When they had finished, they had three sides of a square with their pins in one area and one more pin in a different part of the city. They just stared at the map for a moment.

"This sure looks like it's the same gang. Otherwise, there wouldn't be much chance of a pattern. They must be hitting that fourth corner next!" Max said.

"We don't even know if there's a bank near that corner."

Max scratched his head. Then his face lit up. "We can go check!" he shouted.

"Not until tomorrow!" Mr. Greebly called from down the hall.

Max and Bella put their heads together and whispered. "It's only four o'clock and that area isn't far."

They got up quietly and sneaked towards the rec room door. Max reached out and was about to grab the doorknob when he heard his father's voice again.

"I said tomorrow!"

"He must have this room bugged," Max whispered to Bella.

"I heard that!"

So they played on Max's computer, shooting down bugs that were trying to take over the world. They cleared all the bugs out of Asia and started on Europe. Max and Bella worked as a team and had just cleared the bugs from the Eiffel Tower and the rest of Paris when Max was called for supper and Bella ran home. They planned to meet up after breakfast the next day.

CHAPTER 5

THE NEXT MORNING, BELLA AND MAX WERE LOUNGING in Max's rec room studying their map and the pins that showed where all the banks had been robbed. Three corners of a section of the map had pins, and the fourth corner had no pin in it.

"I still think we should try this one corner," Max said.

"Maybe. But if you look closely, you'll see one more pin which doesn't seem to fit into your pattern. It's on the other end of town. Now what do you suppose that means?"

"I have no idea, but do you want to go spy out this fourth corner?"

"For sure!"

They packed a lunch and some snacks so they wouldn't starve to death, and headed off on their bikes. Cyrus rode along in Max's pocket, happy to be going along.

They arrived at the corner and stopped in front of the drugstore. Sure enough, there was a bank right across the street. They sat on a bench and drank from juice boxes and snacked on trail mix while they waited to see if the bank was going to get robbed. Cyrus munched happily on the pet food Max brought along.

"Are you excited about going back to school?" Bella asked.

"School is okay, but I'm sure not excited. There's too much fun to have yet before school starts!"

"But we're going to be in grade seven! We're moving up in the world."

"Don't you mean down?"

"What do you mean?"

"In grade six, we were the big kids in school. In grade seven we'll be the little kids."

"Hmm, I never thought of that, but still," Bella said with a bright smile, "it will be an adventure!"

Max smiled. "It won't be boring, that's for sure!"

Though they sat there most of the day, no bank robbers appeared. Around four o'clock, a policeman came up to them.

"All right you kids, beat it! There's no loitering here!"

"We're not loitering," Max said. "We're resting."

"You kids have two minutes to get out of here, and then I'm gonna get mad!"

Max put Cyrus back in his pocket. Then he and Bella grabbed their packs, stuffed their remaining snacks inside, zipped them shut and took off on their bikes, leaving the policeman far behind.

That night, Max's mom and dad told him of a new bank robbery. After supper, he found out where that bank had been and put another pin in his map. There were still the three sides of the square and now two pins on the other side of town. Five pins altogether. He took the map up to his room and pinned it to his wall. Then he lay on his bed and stared at the map for a long time.

When he got tired, Max tried to sleep, but he just couldn't. He sat up and turned on his reading lamp. He noticed his open Bible on his bedside table and realized he hadn't read it in a while. He got up and read a few verses, and then he suddenly got an idea.

He pulled out his notebook and flipped to a blank page, then drew a simple spider. Then he stared at the map for a long time until he finally fell asleep.

The next morning after breakfast, Max grabbed Cyrus, stuffed a few things in his backpack and ran out the door.

"Where are you going?" Mrs. Greebly called after him.

"To Bella's!"

When he was safely in Bella's room, Max pulled a map out of his backpack.

"Look, Bella, you're not going to believe this," he said as he spread the map on her desk.

It was a 3D map of downtown. "Look at the courthouse," Max said.

Bella looked but didn't say anything.

"You see how the entrance of the courthouse sticks out from the main building?"

Bella nodded.

"Well, just imagine that the courthouse is the body of a spider and the entrance is its head. Now if we draw a line from it to where all the banks are that have been robbed..."

"They make spider legs!" Bella said breathlessly.

"Maybe the bank robbers will rob another bank next Saturday and we can find out what they look like." Max circled the banks on the map that would complete the spider.

"Since spiders have eight legs, we know there are still three more banks left to rob."

"We just have to figure out which bank they'll rob next!"

CHAPTER 6

THE NEXT SATURDAY, MAX AND BELLA WERE LYING ON their stomachs on a small hill overlooking a bank. Max was using the binoculars he'd won at the fair the year before. They were actually a lot better than he'd thought they would be. He was watching people walk in and out of the bank as they ran their morning errands when a black van pulled up to the curb right in front of the bank and four men with guns got out.

"Bella, they're here!" he whispered.

Bella pulled out her digital camera that she'd gotten for her birthday, zoomed in on their faces, and started taking pictures.

Then the bank robbers were inside the bank. "Bella, get a picture of the van and the license plate." They were very close to the bank. Just on the other side of the street and up a couple buildings. Still, Bella couldn't get a good view of the license plate from where she was.

"I'm going to get a little closer." Bella got up and ran down the small hill and down the block a bit until she could get a good picture of the license plate. She had just taken a couple pictures when one of the bank robbers burst out of the bank and looked around wildly.

His eyes scanned the block on his side of the street, then the opposite side. When he looked past where Bella had been, Max looked too but she was nowhere to be seen. Suddenly she was beside him again.

"Where did you go?"

"Behind the buildings, silly," she said with a smile. "I didn't want to be seen."

She showed him the pictures she'd taken and Max could clearly read the van's license plate.

He looked back up in time to see a huge man come out of the bank. He was wearing a t-shirt stretched tight across his muscles. When he raised an arm to open the van door, Max saw his biceps and shoulder muscles ripple. *He must be incredibly strong*, Max thought.

After the van roared off, Max and Bella went back home. Bella went to her house because she and her mom were going shopping that afternoon. School was only two weeks away and her mom wanted to get her some back-to-school supplies before all the good stuff was gone. But Bella promised to come over after supper.

Mr. Greebly came home from work early, so Max told him what they had seen that morning. Then he went up to visit Cyrus, who looked mad that he hadn't been included in the morning's little adventure. His quills were standing straight up and he just stared at Max. Max had never seen him so mad.

"Sorry, Cyrus, we didn't do anything except take some pictures and watch. Don't worry. There will be plenty of excitement later, and you'll be there."

Max decided to play some video games. As he played, he could feel a pair of eyes burning into his back. Whenever he looked, Cyrus was still staring angrily at him.

Finally, Cyrus gave up, curled up into a ball, and went to sleep. Max relaxed and finally got into his game. Before he knew it, it was suppertime.

After supper when the doorbell rang, Max rushed to open it, excited to have Bella over to discuss the bank robbers. She had an envelope in her hand when he opened the door.

"I got the pictures printed!" she said breathlessly as she bounced into the house.

Max couldn't wait to see them, so they headed to the kitchen table. Mr. Greebly joined them as they spread the pictures over the table.

"The zoom on your camera works really well," Mr. Greebly told her.

The pictures had clear images of all the bank robber's faces as well as the license plate of their getaway van.

"I'd better call Detective Mallory," Mr. Greebly said. "He'll want to see these."

He got up and headed into his den to make the call while Max and Bella continued to stare at each picture, one after another. Suddenly, the doorbell rang. Max's mother opened the door, and moments later Detective Mallory was leaning over the table looking at the pictures.

"You didn't need to come tonight," Mr. Greebly said, coming into the kitchen.

"I needed to see these right away," Detective Mallory said. He tapped the picture of the guy with the huge muscles. "We believe this is the leader. He normally doesn't do the jobs himself, but because of the robbers we put away thanks to Max, he's a little shorthanded right now.

"Good job getting those pictures. It was a bright idea of yours to cover one bank while we covered the other two. That way we couldn't miss them." He smiled down at Max and rested his hand gently on his shoulder.

Just then, Tara burst into the room. "Who was at the door?" she started to ask, then saw

Detective Mallory and the pictures on the table. "Oooh, pictures," she squealed.

Long after the detective and Bella had left, Max stared at the picture of the leader of the gang of bank robbers. The bank where Max and Bella had gotten pictures was the sixth that had been robbed. That only left two banks to complete a picture of a spider with its eight legs.

CHAPTER 7

MAX WAS OUT WALKING IN THE PARK THE NEXT afternoon with Cyrus in his pocket. Bella was busy with her mom again, so Max was just wandering around the park enjoying the day when two men in dark suits and dark sunglasses approached. He was about to run when the men pulled out badges.

"I'm Agent Connors," said the first man with blond hair.

"And I'm Agent Matthews," said the other, who had dark hair and a mustache.

Max just looked at them. He didn't know what to say. Maybe he was under arrest for using marbles to help catch those bank robbers. He could almost see the headline now, *"Boy arrested for illegal use of marbles."*

"Max, we need your help."

How do they know my name? He wondered.

"We've heard how you caught those bank robbers with your marbles and we know you've seen the ringleader. We need some help getting into his house."

"You want *me* to break into his house?" Max asked, his mouth hanging open.

"Not you!"

Max's gaze followed their pointing fingers to his shirt pocket. He couldn't think why they'd want his shirt pocket to break into a house.

"Your pet!" said Agent Connors as if reading his mind.

"I don't even know where the ringleader lives."

"That's okay, because we do, thanks to the picture you got of the license plate," said Agent Connors. "The leader's name is Spider. He comes out of his house every morning at seven o'clock wearing slippers to get his newspaper. He doesn't pay much attention once he picks up his paper so we think your pet...what's his name?"

"Cyrus."

"Right, so we think Cyrus can run up when Spider is heading back into his house and hop up onto his slipper and get a ride right into the house."

"I don't know...I'd have to ask my parents."

"We already talked to your mom," said Agent Matthews, his mustache twitching. "But we can go talk to her with you and explain the plan. How does that sound to you, Max?"

Max nodded and they headed back to his house. His dad was home by this time, but hadn't heard much about the plan so the two men explained it again.

"And Max would be safe the whole time?" Mr. Greebly asked.

"Perfectly safe," said Agent Connors. "He'd be with us a safe distance away."

"Then why do you need Max?"

"Because Max is his owner and Cyrus may not be comfortable going with us without Max. So we need them both."

"Will Cyrus be safe?" Max asked.

"We'll attach a tiny video camera to Cyrus' collar so that we'll know what's happening at all times. If Cyrus is in danger, we'll send our men in to save him," Agent Connors explained.

"Why do you want Cyrus to go into Spider's house?" Mrs. Greebly asked.

"First of all, he's the only one of us that can slip inside. We want to put a tiny video camera and microphone on his collar so that we can find out which bank the robbers are going to rob next," said Agent Matthews.

"Why don't you just plant a bug in the house, instead of taking Max and Cyrus there?" Tara asked, sounding unusually protective of her younger brother.

Max looked at her shocked. He had never thought she cared about him.

"Spider has several men living in the house at all times, so we can't sneak in and plant a bug. Cyrus, though, can go in there and hide and sneak around when no one is looking. Once we've heard where the next bank robbery will be, all Cyrus has to do is leave the house, either by a window or through the door when anyone leaves," said Agent Connors.

"It's important that we catch them at the next robbery or we may never catch them," said Agent Matthews.

Agents Connors and Matthews said they would let Max and Cyrus know when they needed them. For the next three days, Max played with Bella. They spied on the neighbors, sneaking through their yards until they got caught and then running away laughing. When Mrs. Glockner went to take care of her flowers and saw Max and Bella's faces behind her roses, she was so shocked she almost fell over.

That's when Max and Bella jumped up laughing and ran away into the next neighbor's yard. Max tried to avoid Mr. Harvey's place, but when they were surprised by a dog that rushed at them in the Parsons' yard, they ran around screaming until they ended up in the next yard and the dog's leash wouldn't reach that far. The dog gave up and went in search of his bone.

"I didn't know the Parsons had a dog," Max said, catching his breath.

"Me either!" Bella said, flopping on her back with her arms and legs spread out.

Max did the same and closed his eyes while he enjoyed the warm air and the nice breeze and waited for his heart to stop pounding.

A minute later, a shadow passed overhead and blocked the sun. Max opened his eyes and looked right at the big bushy eyebrows of Mr. Harvey.

"What are you kids doing in my yard?"

"We were running from the dog in the Parsons' yard," Bella told him.

Mr. Harvey held his hand out to Max, palm up. "Look what your pet left on my lawn."

Max sat up a little and peered into Mr. Harvey's hand. He could only see some black dots.

"They're really small. Do you have a magnifying glass?"

Mr. Harvey just glared at him, waiting for an answer.

"Dead ants?"

"No!" Mr. Harvey roared. "Your pet left these on my lawn."

"Mud from his feet?"

"Look closer!" Mr. Harvey shoved his hand up to Max's face so his eye was only an inch away from whatever he was holding.

"It looks like dirt from your flower bed. You'd better wash your hands."

Max wasn't trying to be rude, but the things in Mr. Harvey's hand were so small he wasn't sure what he was seeing. Plus, why would he get so excited about something that small on his lawn?

"Your pet rodent pooped on my lawn!"

"Cyrus is a hedgehog, not a rodent!" Max yelled back.

"Yeah!" said Bella.

"He's a rodent!"

So Max sat Mr. Harvey down and explained it all to him. "...Rodents belong to the Order *Rodentia* and the hedgehog belongs to the Order *Erinaceomorpha*."

"Arggggg!"

Mr. Harvey jumped up and stormed back to his house.

Maybe I should have asked Mr. Harvey if he had a microscope instead, Max thought. *Those things in his hand were awfully small—that's probably the only way to really identify those tiny things he was holding.*

"Come on, Bella. Let's go before Mr. Harvey comes back and asks us more questions!" Max said.

Max and Bella got up and bolted, running as fast as they could out of Mr. Harvey's yard and into Max's.

"He's crazy," Bella whispered.

"That's for sure!" Max whispered back. "It feels like he's watching us! Let's go inside!" Max made a mad dash for his house with Bella right behind him.

When they had the door closed behind them and had run to the living room, they finally felt safe. Max lay on the floor while Bella flopped onto the sofa. Then they let their minds wander while they recovered from the Parsons' dog and Mr. Harvey with the microscopic dots in his hand.

After a while, Bella quickly sat up. "Josh is coming home tomorrow!"

Max sat bolt upright, too. "He's been gone forever!"

"A month and half. He is so lucky!"

CHAPTER 8

"JOSH!" BELLA SCREAMED AS SHE RAN DOWN THE sidewalk to where Josh was just climbing out of his parents' motor home.

"Hi, Bella," he said shyly.

She gave him a big hug, then they started walking towards Max's house. They were just two doors down when Max flew out of the house, saw Josh and Bella and skidded to a stop. "Hey, Josh," he said, waving.

"So tell us where you went on your trip," Bella said.

"The Grand Canyon, San Francisco, Disneyland—"

"What was Disneyland like?" Max asked excitedly.

"The rides were awesome. I liked the roller-coaster next door in the Disney California Adventure Park called California Screamin'. I liked it best because my mom and dad didn't like it at all. So I got to go on it alone. I went on it nine times!"

They headed into Max's house to visit.

"So what was the Grand Canyon like?" Max asked.

"Big. I scared my parents so bad because I wanted to jump to this rock and that rock." Josh smiled. "They made me stay on the path after that."

"What was the best part?" Bella asked.

"Oh, we took a helicopter tour and that was so cool! My stomach dropped when we first flew over the rim and there was the floor of the canyon a mile down.

"My mom and dad had a big breakfast and they had to use the barf bags when we were looking down a mile to the floor of the canyon." Josh laughed. Then he groaned. "I forgot about my parents. They'll need my help to unload the RV. I gotta go! See you guys later?"

"Sure, just come over when you're free," Max said.

"Who wants a sundae?" Mr. Greebly asked after supper.

"I do!" Max and Tara said at the same time.

Max loved sundaes with ice cream, nuts, chocolate sprinkles, and chocolate sauce.

School started on Monday, so the family

was having sundaes to celebrate the last night of summer vacation. There were plenty of sprinkles to go around.

The next morning, Max, Bella, and Josh walked to their new school together. They were starting grade seven in the junior high school in town, and didn't know what to expect.

The first thing they did was find their lockers, which were pretty close together. They stuffed their belongings in them, got their books for the first class, and were heading there when they saw a shocking sight: a person who looked more like gorilla than a human.

"Who's that?" they whispered to a girl who was standing close by.

"Oh that's Snarl," she replied. "He's failed grade eight three times, I hear. The guy next to him who looks like an elf is his buddy Carl. They are the school bullies."

"The little boy actually bullies people?" Max found that a little hard to believe.

"He never goes anywhere without Snarl, so people do what he says. But Snarl is the leader, and since he's so big, people really do what he says and not so much what Carl says."

The three of them watched Snarl and Carl bully a young boy into giving up a handful of change. He then ran off while Snarl counted the money.

Just then, a buzzer went off.

"That's the warning bell," the girl beside them said as she started walking off. "If you aren't in class before the next buzzer you'll get in trouble," she said over her shoulder as she hurried away.

Max and his two buddies hurried to their first class. They had all the same classes, since they were all new in the junior high school. They wanted to stick together at least until they all felt comfortable.

After school, they all walked home together. "See you guys tomorrow," Josh said as he ran off.

"What's he so excited about?" Max asked, thinking out loud.

"He wants to work on his room and get all his things unpacked and put away so that it'll feel like a bedroom," Bella explained.

"When did you find that out?"

"Today at school."

"We were together all day. I don't remember Josh saying that!"

"He told me when you were distracted by that cute girl, Mindy," Bella said, teasing him.

"I just wanted to talk to her!" Max said defensively.

"Oh, I know!" Bella said as she punched him lightly in the arm. Then she started running home. "Call me if anything exciting happens at your place! I don't want to miss anything!"

CHAPTER 9

JOSH AND BELLA WERE OVER AT MAX'S HOUSE THAT evening. They were playing computer games in the rec room when the doorbell rang. They looked out the window and saw a dark sedan parked at the curb.

"Max, can you come up here?" Mr. Greebly called from upstairs.

"Come on, guys, let's go see who it is," Max said. They all ran up the stairs and arrived in a group at the top. The two agents from the other week were there, still wearing dark suits and dark sunglasses.

"Hello, Max," they both said. "Are these your friends?"

"Yes, this is Bella. She lives a couple doors down. And this is Josh. He lives down the block."

"It's nice to meet you," said Blondie and Mustache Man. Then they got serious and looked at Max. "We need to talk to you and your parents alone."

"I want my friends to hear this, too," Max said. He looked to his parents for support.

"It can't hurt, can it?" Mr. Greebly asked the agents.

They shrugged. "I guess not," Agent Connors, the blond agent, said.

They all went into the kitchen, including Cyrus, and sat around the table. Even Tara joined them, for as she said, "I'm not gonna have Max's baby-faced friends hearing everything and not hear it myself!"

Everyone listened as the agents took turns outlining the plan.

"We're going to do this on Saturday, so in just a few days. Are you clear on the plan, Max?"

"I sure am!"

"Do you think Cyrus understands?"

Cyrus nodded vigorously.

"There's your answer," Mr. Greebly said.

"Good. We'll pick you up Saturday and set up Cyrus with the microphone and miniature camera so we can see whatever he sees."

Then the two agents were gone and Max, Tara, their parents, Bella, and Josh talked excitedly amongst themselves. Soon it was time for Bella and Josh to go home and Max and Tara to start heading for bed.

A few days later, Max was yawning as he sat in English class late in the afternoon. He still had his sunglasses on to shade his eyes from the sun pouring in the windows. It was very warm in class and his eyes slowly drooped closed.

He started dreaming about the bank robbers. He was once again with Cyrus, knocking them all down with his marbles. In his dream, one of the robbers had gotten past all the marbles and was standing in front of him.

"Why are you wearing sunglasses, Max?"

"Because the sun is bright," he said, wondering how the bank robber knew his name.

"Take them off and give them to me!"

"No way! The police will be here any minute and then you'll be in trouble!" he said and laughed. By now he could hear the sirens. The police were almost there. "If you want them so bad, you'll have to pry them off my face!"

Suddenly, he felt hands yanking off his sunglasses.

He blinked his eyes open and realized he'd been dreaming.

I hope I didn't say any of those things out loud, he thought.

That's when he noticed that all the kids were laughing and Miss Madison (who they called The Mallet) looked mad enough to take on an angry bull.

Max slipped lower in his seat and prayed the bell would ring to put him out of his misery. But it didn't, and The Mallet went back to teaching the class.

"Since today is Friday, I want you to write me a story about anything you like and have it finished and handed in on Monday. Make sure it's at least one full page long."

When the final bell rang, Max bolted from his seat as if his pants were on fire and took off out of the room, down the hall, and out of the school. He joined up with Josh and Bella and they headed home together.

"Man, that must have been embarrassing!" Josh said. "But that was the funniest thing I've ever seen. When you told The Mallet that if she wanted your sunglasses she was going to have to pry them off your face, I thought I was never going to stop laughing!"

"Give him a break, Josh," said Bella. "He was asleep and dreaming. It could have happened to any of us. I was having a hard time staying awake until that happened. So thanks, Max, you saved me from maybe embarrassing myself."

When Max got home, he felt like working on his homework, so he started writing his story.

Some days I'm not so bright. In fact the other day when I was getting ice cubes out of the freezer I licked the side of the metal tray and got my tongue frozen to it.

I had to run it under the faucet while it dangled from my tongue and I said things like, "Ow, ow, urry it eally urts."

Eventually the water warmed up my tongue and the tray and I was free, but I still talked funny for a few days.

On family vacation I was so embarrassed when I got my foot stuck in a trap, that was dangling eight feet off the ground tied to a high branch of a tree. I refused to explain how I got stuck after my family found me from all my hollering and set me loose. They *needed to get a long ladder to reach me.*

We went to the hot springs and I went to get out of the hot pool and go into the cold pool, but as I jumped up, and got three quarters of my body out of the water so that I could pull himself out, my trunks slid down a bit. I quickly dropped back into the pool but heard some girls laughing. It was horrible. We may never go back.

"Max! Supper!" his mom called from the kitchen.

Max quickly shut down the computer and ran downstairs to find out what exciting things there were to eat.

They had his favorite meal for supper. Barbecued chicken, mashed potatoes, corn and, for dessert, chocolate pudding. Afterwards he lay for an hour on the couch resting his full stomach while his dad watched the baseball game. At halftime, Max's stomach felt good so he ran upstairs to finish his story.

He turned on his computer and continued writing.

The next day we went for a hike thinking that I couldn't possibly embarrass myself in the forest. Boy were we wrong.

"Hey Max, look at these cool nuts!" Tara called out.

We all went to look and saw a cluster of things that might have been nuts. I picked one up and felt it, then I smelled it.

"Yuck!" I said and hurled it far into the forest.

That's when I noticed that there was a group of hikers who had stopped to watch and Tara was on the ground killing herself laughing. Turned out those weren't nuts, they were deer droppings!

CHAPTER 10

"DID THIS REALLY HAPPEN, MAX?" THE MALLET ASKED on Monday. She stood at the front of the class having just read his story aloud amidst roars of laughter.

"No, I made it all up."

"Well, that was a very funny story, Max." He couldn't believe his ears. "Good job!" The Mallet said, and then she smiled.

The whole class sucked in their breath. They had never seen her smile. In fact, some of the students had older brothers and sisters who had been in The Mallet's class and they had never seen her smile, either.

Max got an A on his assignment and he couldn't wait to show it off at home.

"I never made you pick up deer droppings!" Tara yelled after reading Max's story.

"I know that! I made that story up!"

"Now you two," their mother said, "cut it out. Your dad is resting and we all know Max made up the story. Why don't you go spend some time doing something on your own until supper?"

Max headed off to his room and Tara went into the living room to watch TV.

Later, Bella came over because she wanted to read Max's story again. She laughed all the way through it, so hard her stomach muscles were sore by the time she finished.

"That was so funny, Max!"

"Thanks," Max said with a shy smile. He wasn't used to having his homework read by anyone. Certainly, no one had ever asked to read it before.

The next day at school, Mindy came up to him. "I really liked your story from yesterday," she said. "Maybe we could sit at lunch today...?"

Max was stunned. He didn't know what to say. "Uh...um...uh," was all he managed.

"Bring your two friends and join me at my table."

"Uh...okay."

Mindy smiled sweetly at him. "See you later then." She turned and headed off down the hall. Bella and Josh were waiting for him just a short ways away.

"What did she want?" Josh asked.

"She wants us to join her at lunch," Max told them.

"Ooh," Bella said.

"Cut it out!" Max yelled.

Bella smiled.

Max had math just before lunch. The class was halfway through when he had to go to the restroom. He put up his hand.

"Yes, Max? Have you solved the problem I wrote on the board?" Mr. Hardy asked.

"No, sir, but can I go to the bathroom?"

"Fine, go ahead." Mr. Hardy walked to his desk, opened the top drawer, and handed Max a hall pass as he went by.

When Max finished in the restroom, he washed and dried his hands. He was walking down the hall on his way back to class when Snarl and Carl came around the corner and almost ran into him.

"Well, who do we have here?" Snarl said.

They cornered him against the lockers as they looked him over. "If you hand it over, we won't rough you up," Carl piped up.

"Hand over what?"

"Now, don't play dumb, just hand it over," Snarl said, poking a finger into Max's chest.

"Your lunch money, grub! Hand over your lunch money!" Carl said. He was very short, and

Snarl was so close to Max, that Carl had to peek around Snarl's arms.

"Yeah, your lunch money!" Snarl echoed.

"But I only have enough to buy my lunch. I don't have any extra."

"Let's see," Snarl said.

Max dug the money out of his pocket, a difficult task with Snarl so close to him, and showed it to them.

Snarl and Carl looked at the money. "Yep, that is just enough money to buy lunch," Snarl told him.

"Not a penny more," Carl said.

Snarl snatched the money out of Max's hand. "Thanks dude." The two took off, leaving Max standing alone in the hall. He felt like crying.

"Snarl isn't very nice," he said to himself.

When he got back to class, he was startled when Mr. Hardy asked him a question.

"So, did you solve it?"

Max had no idea what he was talking about. "Solve what?" Max asked.

"The math problem on the board. You were gone a long time. Didn't you solve the problem while you were gone?"

All Max could think of was having his lunch money taken away, so he mumbled a reply and didn't hear much of what Mr. Hardy said after that.

At lunch, Max, Bella, and Josh found Mindy's table. Bella and Josh sat down and Max was about to sit beside them when Mindy spoke up. "I saved you a seat beside me, Max."

"Uh...okay." He took the seat she had saved.

"Where's your lunch?" she asked.

"Snarl and Carl stole my lunch money," he said and again felt like crying.

"I'm so sorry, Max," Bella said softly.

"Don't feel bad," Mindy said. "It's happened to practically everyone here. Don't worry, my mom made me a big lunch and there's no way I can eat it all. I'll share it with you."

"That's okay, I'll be alright."

"Please, Max, you'd be doing me a favor. There really is no way I can eat it all. Do you like peanut butter sandwiches?"

"Yes," Max said faintly.

"Good, because my mom made me two. Here, you can have this one." She handed him a sandwich wrapped in a baggie.

The other three made small talk while Max enjoyed the peanut butter sandwich. By the time he was finished, he was feeling much better.

"My mom gave me two puddings. Do you like chocolate?" Mindy asked.

"Yes!" Max actually loved chocolate pudding.

After he'd had a sandwich, a chocolate pudding, a granola bar, and a bottle of orange juice, Max was feeling comfortably full. "Thanks, Mindy."

"Anytime, Max. Do you guys want to join me for lunch tomorrow?" she asked, looking at all three of them.

"We'd love to," Max said. "Right guys?"

Josh and Bella both nodded.

CHAPTER 11

THAT NIGHT, MAX SAID A PRAYER. "PLEASE HELP SNARL to be nicer." Then he shut off his light and went to bed. While he slept, he dreamed he was flying. He often flew in his dreams, but not always. He was zipping around like Iron Man, staying close to the ground until he came up to a tall building. Then he'd pull up so he was flying straight up until he was over the building, then he'd zip down close to the ground again.

When he tired of flying, he landed and immediately Snarl and Carl from school appeared. "Where do you think you're going?" Snarl asked, pushing Max in the chest.

"Yeah, where do you think you're going?" asked Carl.

"Give us your lunch money!" they demanded.

Max searched his pockets but he didn't have any lunch money.

"I...I don't have any money today," he whimpered.

"What do you mean you don't have any lunch money? You always have lunch money. How else are you gonna eat?" Snarl said, getting angry.

Max pulled off the backpack he now realized he was wearing and searched inside. "I've got this!" He held up a soggy jam and peanut butter sandwich.

Snarl knocked it out of his hand. "I don't want that! Give me what I want!"

Max stood up on shaking knees. He wanted to fly away but Snarl and Carl were right in front of him. Their noses almost touched they were so close.

"Give me what I want!" Snarl's voice echoed in his head. Over and over it echoed.

Max woke up. *What was that dream all about?* "What a lousy dream," he said aloud, then rolled over and fell into a restful sleep.

When he woke to his alarm hours later, he turned it off and got out of bed.

Down in the kitchen, his mom asked, "Who were you talking to in your room during the night, Max?"

"Last night? I wasn't talk...oh that! I had a bad dream, I guess."

He had breakfast, then got ready. When it was time, he met Josh and Bella and they headed to school.

At school, Max hurried to his locker, got his books, hung up his jacket, and was walking quickly to class with Bella and Josh when they spotted Snarl and Carl pushing around a smaller boy. Max looked away—he couldn't stand to see that sort of thing—and headed to class.

At lunch, Max, Josh, and Bella joined Mindy at her table. Mindy had again saved a seat beside her for Max.

"Hi Max!" she said happily when she spotted him. She patted the seat next to her and then waved Bella and Josh into two empty seats across the table.

"Did you have any trouble with those nasty boys Snarl and Carl today?"

"Not today," Max said. "Have you ever had any trouble with them?"

"Thank goodness, no." Mindy leaned closer to Max and softly said, "I think they both like me and so they leave me alone. They do sometimes follow me around like little puppy dogs, but they never try to take my lunch money. Which is a good thing, because I bring my own lunch every day and wouldn't have a penny to give them."

In English class that afternoon, The Mallet gave them a new assignment. "I want you to make up a newspaper headline that will grab everyone's attention and then write a short, interesting article. Between one hundred and 150 words should be long enough. You may begin now."

The first thing that jumped into Max's head was:

SOCK SNIFFERS UNITE!

Max wrote that down at the very top of a new page in his English notebook. Then he sat and thought what he could write about it.

"Has everyone written a headline?" The Mallet asked.

Everyone in the class looked up and just stared at her.

"Maybe I should put it this way: has anyone not written a headline?"

No hands went up.

"Okay...Mindy, what have you written?"

"Bear mauls hotdog stand," Mindy said.

"Good. How about you, Josh?"

"Uh, chicken slips on ice, slams its head."

"That's good, Josh!" The Mallet had been a lot nicer ever since Max's story made her smile. "Max? What do you have for us?"

"It's silly," Max said softly.

"Come now, don't be shy. It can't be that silly."

"I don't know..."

"Just read it to us, Max!" The Mallet ordered.

"Well, okay...sock sniffers unite..."

"That's good, Max. It makes me want to read it just to find out what it's all about."

Max smiled and felt better about his headline. Just then the buzzer went.

"I want you to write your article and hand it in next week," The Mallet called out as everyone was shuffling out the door to their next class.

CHAPTER 12

ON SATURDAY, AGENTS CONNORS AND MATTHEWS showed up and Max and Cyrus went with them to Spider's house. Mr. Greebly came along, too, so he could be with Max while Cyrus was in Spider's house.

When they arrived at the house and had hooked up a tiny camera and microphone to a special collar they'd made for Cyrus, they let Cyrus out and he ran and hid between the newspaper lying on the sidewalk and the front door of the house.

At exactly seven o'clock, Spider came out to get the newspaper. The agents watched from inside the van with binoculars. Spider's hair was messy, as if he had just gotten up. He was wearing a robe stretched tight by his large muscles and he had on bright pink bunny slippers that squeaked as he walked.

Squeak
Squeak
Squeak

Down the front path he went, until he got to his newspaper and bent over and picked it up. He then turned around and squeak, squeak, squeaked his way back to his house.

Spider was halfway back to his door, reading the front page of the newspaper when Max saw Cyrus dart out from between some bushes and do a flying leap onto Spider's slipper.

Then Spider was at his door. He opened it and went in, and the last thing Max saw was Cyrus hanging on to the pink slipper's bunny ears.

Back in the van, the agents turned on their little TV. Soon a picture came up of the inside of the house. Cyrus was still going up and down on Spider's slipper, and watching the motion was making them all a little sick.

When Cyrus got tired of his up-and-down ride, he looked for a place to get off. Soon he saw some soft carpet coming up. When he got to it, he tucked and rolled and came up under a chair.

He waited and watched.

Cyrus saw men coming and going in many different directions and he figured out where the kitchen was when he saw men going in empty-handed and coming out with food. His stomach growled and he eyed the food hungrily.

"Hey Merv, have you seen my sandwich?"

"I have better things to do than watch your sandwich, Harley! I have my own food!"

"Bill, give me back my chips!"

"I don't have your rotten chips, Pierce!"

"You're lying! I can hear you over there munching on them!"

The munching stopped.

Cyrus watched as Pierce walked around the corner towards him. When he got to Bill, the two started slugging it out.

Bill gave Pierce an uppercut to the jaw, and Pierce went flying backward and landed against the coffee table. He got up slowly and when Bill got close enough to hit him again, Pierce hit Bill with the coffee table, knocking him over. Then Pierce started to sway and collapsed on the floor, where they both groaned and then blacked out.

Cyrus watched the two of them for a minute from his hiding place in the corner. Then went back to eating Pierce's chips.

When he was finished, he ran off to another part of the house. Here he found more men keeping watch out the windows with binoculars. One man had put his binoculars down and was eating a chocolate bar. Suddenly he threw the chocolate bar towards the chair and grabbed at his binoculars. Whatever it was must have been nothing, because he went to put his binocs back down and get his chocolate bar.

But it was gone!

"Hey Stu, you seen my chocolate bar?"

"Now how would I see it, Fred? I'm way over here on the other side of the room."

"You stole it when that van went roaring past the house!"

Cyrus had been very happy when Fred threw his candy bar. It hit the chair, bounced over the arm, and landed on the floor. Cyrus just couldn't resist. After eating Harley's sandwich and snacking on Pierce's potato chips, Cyrus really wanted some dessert, so he dragged the chocolate bar away to eat in peace.

After polishing off the chocolate, Cyrus was sleepy, so he curled up and took a nice nap.

He woke quickly a few minutes later when he heard Spider yell, "What are you two doing?"

Fred had his big hands around Stu's throat. The two were locked in battle. Fred let go when he heard Spider yelling.

"He stole my chocolate bar, boss."

"I don't care about your candy!" Spider roared. "We have a meeting downstairs. Get all the guys together and meet me there." Spider turned on his heel and walked away.

Since Cyrus didn't know where the basement was, he followed Fred and Stu. He saw when they found Pierce and Bill lying unconscious on the floor.

After a few light slaps to the face, Pierce and Bill woke up.

"What happened to you guys?" Stu said in a hoarse croak.

"He stole my chips!" Pierce said. "What happened to your voice?"

"Fred tried to strangle me."

Bill looked at Fred for a minute.

"Well he stole my chocolate!" Fred said defensively.

"Something weird is going on here," Bill said.

They staggered to their feet and followed Stu and Fred as they rounded up the rest of the guys. Then they headed to the basement, but none of them saw Cyrus sneaking along behind them.

Cyrus darted from place to place so he wouldn't be seen. After a while he felt silly doing that and just followed the men. They kept going down flight after flight of stairs.

This is one deep basement, he thought.

Down and down they went until the walls of the house disappeared and Cyrus saw rock walls. Finally, he came to a place where he could see the bottom and about ten feet above the floor, he saw a beam as long as the room. When he got down to that level, he ran out across the beam until he was looking straight down at the group of men gathered around a table.

Everyone in the van saw only a dark room, but they could hear voices speaking.

"Wonder what the boss wants to tell us today?" one voice said.

"Okay boys, we have one more bank robbery to do and then we're finished."

They heard crinkling paper and suddenly the camera was moving and then it was looking straight down. They all saw a map of the city laid out with a light shining on it.

Then a huge man with wide, muscled shoulders pointed his finger at a spot on the map.

"That must be Spider," Agent Matthews said.

"We'll hit this bank on November 30, a Saturday. It's only a week and a half away, so I want all of you to lie low and meet up at my place at nine o'clock in the morning that day.

"I thought we had two more banks to rob," one of the men said.

"That's what I want the police to think. But we're gonna rob one more bank and then we're gonna disappear," Spider explained.

Spider looked around to make sure they all understood.

"Okay. Go home, and I don't want to see you again until then."

About twenty minutes later, Max and everyone in the van saw a man come out of the house, then another and another.

Looking back to the TV screen, they could see from the camera on Cyrus that he was heading towards the front door.

They watched the door and when the next man came out, Max saw Cyrus dive out the door, land on his feet, and roll into the bushes.

Once Cyrus was safely in the van, the agents dropped Max, Cyrus, and Mr. Greebly back at their house.

"Max, you must promise us that you'll stay far away from the next bank robbery and let us handle it," Agent Connors said.

"But I want to see these robbers get caught!"

"It'll be on the news. So maybe your parents will let you watch the news that night."

The agents left, and Max spent the rest of the weekend playing with Josh and Bella.

CHAPTER 13

A COUPLE DAYS LATER AT SCHOOL, SNARL AND CARL again cornered Max.

"Hand it over, punk!"

Max had been through this before. Instead of asking what they wanted him to hand over, he thought he'd try confusing them.

"You have a bee on you!" he yelled.

"Eeeeek," said Snarl, jumping around. Carl screamed like a girl and jumped right into Snarl's arms.

By the time they realized there was no bee, Max was nowhere to be seen.

On the way out of school at the end of the day, Max, Bella, and Josh bumped into Mindy.

"Hi, guys!" she said. "Are you interested in working on our newspaper articles together tonight?"

Max, Josh, and Bella all looked at each other. Then Bella shrugged. "Sure, why not. Where should we do this?"

"You can come to my house," Max said. "Does seven o'clock work for everyone?"

Everyone agreed and Max told Mindy where he lived, since she had never been there before.

Mindy went her way and Max, Josh, and Bella headed off home together.

"See you later," Bella and Josh said when they got to Max's house.

After supper, the Greeblys had root beer floats. Mr. Greebly was telling a story about going camping when he was a boy. "We were sitting around the campfire and my parents were telling me about leeches and how when they get on you they attach themselves to you and suck your blood. I started feeling things crawling all over me when I heard that, and when I felt something running across my leg, I screamed.

"My dad turned on the flashlight and swept the beam over my leg. And do you know what he found crawling on me?"

"No, tell us!" Max and Tara said in unison.

"It was a cute itty bitty ladybug!"

CHAPTER 14

AT SEVEN O'CLOCK THAT NIGHT, JOSH AND MINDY showed up at Max's house a few minutes apart.

"Where's Bella?" Mindy asked.

"She called to say she won't be coming tonight. Her cat had kittens and she wanted to stay home and watch them," Max said.

The three of them headed to the dining room, sat around the table, and got ready to write their newspaper articles.

An hour later, they were all finished.

"Man, that was hard," Josh said. "But once I got an idea of what to write, it went pretty fast!"

"Do you want to play a game?" Max asked.

"Max," his mother called, "you have chores to do. Time for your friends to go home."

Josh took his newspaper article, got his shoes, and headed out. "See you tomorrow!" he said.

"See ya," Max replied.

Mindy was just tying her shoes when Josh left. She stood when she was finished and smiled at Max. "See you tomorrow?"

"You bet."

"I'd love to read your article if The Mallet doesn't read it to the class. I think you're very funny."

Then she went out the door and Max closed it after her.

"What chores do I need to do, Mom?"

"You need to clean Cyrus's cage and then take a shower," she called back.

"Again? I just cleaned his cage."

"That was a couple weeks ago."

Max headed to his room, opened the cage, and picked up Cyrus.

"When are you going to learn to clean your own cage?"

Cyrus just glared at him.

Max was almost to the bathroom when Tara ran out of her room, slipped past him and ran into the bathroom, slamming the door behind her.

Max banged on the bathroom door.

"Go away," Tara said.

"I was just going into the bathroom to put Cyrus in the bathtub so he wouldn't run away while I cleaned his cage," Max said.

"Too bad! Put him on your bed."

So Max did. He got Cyrus' cage cleaned and then when Tara was finished in the bathroom, he took a shower and went to bed.

The next day in class, The Mallet collected all the newspaper articles. "Now, I'll grade all these tonight, but I'd like Josh, Mindy, and Max to read their articles out loud to the class."

Everyone cheered.

"Okay, Mindy, why don't you start?" The Mallet said.

Mindy got up, cleared her throat, and read:

BEAR ATTACKS HOTDOG STAND

A hungry bear today attacked a hotdog stand downtown. The scared owner ran off to call the police. When the police arrived, they found the bear had ripped open the side of the stand and had devoured all the ketchup and mustard. The bear was lying on its back moaning with a ketchup mustache and a mustard beard. The police had the bear transported to a vet who said the only thing the bear was suffering from was a giant tummy ache.

The bear has been released back into the wild but recently there have been other reports of a bear attacking hotdog stands in the area.

"Very good, Mindy. Okay Josh, why don't you go next."

Josh got up and read:

CHICKEN SLIPS ON ICE,
SLAMS ITS HEAD

Residents of Elfville saw a strange sight last winter, when they saw a chicken, slipping and sliding down the icy main street. It bounced off cars, tripped over curbs, and got some serious air off snow drifts. One drift was quite large and just before the chicken got to it a big gust of wind came up and blew that chicken up the snow pile so high that it slammed into a window on the third story of an office building scaring all the people inside. Then it slid slowly down the window with its tongue sticking out until it fell and slammed it's head into a deep snow bank. Last seen it was staggering down main street.

The class cheered.

"That was very good, Josh. All right, Max, you're up."

Max got up, shuffled to the front of the class, and read:

SOCK SNIFFERS UNITE

Sock Sniffers from Canada and the United States gathered together in Los

Angeles for the first ever official meeting in this group's short existence. From far and wide they came, these people who are addicted to smelling their own socks. They find the smell intoxicating. They all came together to share stories and have big group hugs. Shunned by society they met here today for the very first time and talked about their socks smelling like walnuts and cotton candy. When interviewed some of the people had this to say, "I like dem der socks. Dey smell yummy!"

Everyone laughed, and then the school bell rang.

CHAPTER 15

SNARL AND CARL HAD MAX PINNED AGAINST HIS LOCKER.
"Where's your lunch money, Greebly? You're not gonna fool us like you did last time!"

"I don't have it today. My mom made me a lunch."

"Now why would she do something dumb like that?"

"Uh, because she wants me to eat healthy..."

Snarl grabbed Max by the shirt and pulled him forward until their noses were touching.

"You've got a booger in your nose," Max told Snarl, trying to distract him.

Snarl immediately let go of Max and felt his nose.

"There's nothing there!" Snarl yelled.

"You mean your nose is completely empty?" Max asked.

"Are you making fun of me?"

"You have something in your shoe!" Max yelled.

Confused, Snarl looked down. "That's my foot in my shoe, you little creep! What kind of game are you playing? Where's your lunch money?"

"I told you, I don't have any today."

Just then, the principal walked up. "You boys better get to class. It's about to begin."

Snarl let go of Max's shirt and Max slipped away and hurried to his class.

The day of the bank robbery, Bella and Max were bored. Josh was busy with his family, and they were sitting on Max's front porch wondering what to do.

"I wish we could have watched the police catch the bank robbers!" Max said. "I could have brought my marbles in case they needed help."

"It would have been nice, but it's got to be over by now. It's two o'clock in the afternoon and the robbery was supposed to be at nine. You told me so yourself!"

"You're right..." Max said. "Let's go ask my parents if I can watch the six o'clock news."

They ran into the house and Max found his mom and dad relaxing in the living room.

"You know you're not allowed to watch the evening news," his dad told them. Then he winked at Bella.

"But since you helped the police so much, we'll turn on the news and when it gets to the part you want to watch, we'll call you," Max's mom said.

"Woo hoo!" Max yelled as he and Bella ran down to the rec room.

"Let's play a game," Max said.

"How about Bug Zapper? We were right in the middle of it last time."

They loaded that game and sat down to play. They started back in Spain, and killed all the bugs before moving on to Africa.

In the northern part of the continent, they were fighting the nasty bugs in the Sahara desert. The bugs hid in the valleys and in the mountains. Max and Bella fought hard and made it to the south end of the desert, where the bugs hid in the sand dunes.

"Man, these bugs are hard to find in the dunes!" Bella said.

"They sure are!" Max said with gritted teeth as he shot another one.

They were still hunting bugs in the sand dunes when Max's mom announced supper. It was five o'clock.

"Ask your mom if you can come over and watch the news with us," Max said.

"Okay," Bella replied.

Bella headed home for supper and Max headed to the kitchen.

After supper, Max was helping his mother load the dishwasher when Bella came back over.

She had just come in the door when Mr. Greebly called out, "It's starting!"

Max and Bella raced into the living room just in time to hear the news anchor announce, "Here is some video from early this morning."

Max's whole family had come into the living room, and they saw the front of a bank. A man wearing a ski mask burst out of the bank and right into the waiting arms of the police. He was hauled off kicking and screaming to a waiting police car and put into the back seat.

A second man wearing a ski mask ran out of the bank, saw the police waiting for him, and managed to turn and run down the sidewalk. Two police dogs were released and they ran after the man, who squealed like a pig as he tried to outrun them. Finally, one of the dogs leaped into the air and hit the man in the back, sending him flying. The bag of money he was carrying burst open and the police officers who had caught up ran wildly around trying to catch the money.

Eventually they got all the money and then released the robber who was still pinned to the ground by the two dogs. They handcuffed him and led him off to the police cars.

"I want my mommy!" the robber cried.

A third and fourth bank robber came out of the bank. They saw what had happened to their pals and tried to run back into the bank, but one brave officer did a running leap and kicked the door to the bank shut.

They were quickly handcuffed and put in the back of second police car.

A fifth man peeked his head out of the door, then made a run for it. He actually slid over the hood of a police car, ran across the street and then dashed around the corner.

The TV screen switched from the scene of the bank robbery back to the news lady sitting at her desk.

"That robber actually climbed up a drain pipe to the roof of a building. It took the police half an hour to finally catch him. Now back to the video."

Another bank robber emerged from the bank. His broad shoulders filled the doorway as he looked around. Then he started walking down the sidewalk.

"That's Spider," Max whispered.

Two police officers tried to tackle him, but he swatted them away as if they were flies.

It eventually took ten big policemen to take him down and get him handcuffed. They actually carried him to a third police car and put him in the back seat.

The TV screen switched again back to the newsroom. "When asked, the police said they carried the man known as Spider to the police car because they had such a hard time taking him down the first time that they didn't want him to get back on his feet again.

"Two more bank robbers gave up when the police stormed the bank."

The next weekend, Max, Cyrus, and Bella were honored by the Mayor and by the banks.

"Max Greebly, for going above and beyond your normal duty, and for helping the police catch that gang of bank robbers, we and the banks are pleased to give you this medal for bravery and a check for twenty thousand dollars."

They also gave a medal and big check to Bella. Although it was not as big a check as Max got, it was still very nice.

Cyrus even got a tiny little medal to hang around his neck. He wore it proudly.

CHAPTER 16

THAT MONDAY, THE WHOLE SCHOOL WAS BUZZING when Max, Bella, and Josh arrived. Everyone was talking about the rewards Bella and Max had gotten.

"What are you going to do with the money?" someone asked Max.

"My parents are going to keep it for me until I'm old enough," Max explained.

"That's too bad!" someone else called out from the group that had formed around Max.

There were plenty of back slaps and congratulations to go around for both Max and Bella.

Several days later, when Max, Bella, and Josh got to school, the students were all in small groups talking in hushed tones.

Max and his friends heard little pieces of conversations as they walked past.

"Snarl is in the hospital," they heard someone say.

"Two broken legs."

"I hear he's in the General Hospital."

"I heard that Carl hasn't even visited him."

That night, Max told his parents about Snarl and what had happened to him.

"He steals my lunch money! It's weird, though. I had a dream about Snarl trying to steal my lunch money, but I didn't have any, just a soggy sandwich. But in the dream Snarl yelled, 'Give me what I want!'

"I keep hearing those words in my head. I can't get it to stop!"

"He's probably lonely," Mrs. Greebly said. "Maybe what he needs is a good friend who'll visit him."

"You should visit him," said Mr. Greebly.

"But I can't stand that guy!" Max blurted out.

"If you were in the hospital, wouldn't you want someone to visit you?"

"Not him!"

"What if no one else visited you?"

Max thought about that all the next day, and was still thinking about it that night alone in his bedroom. He didn't know what to do. He spotted his open Bible. He looked at the open page and saw a verse that touched his heart. The next day, he decided to go visit Snarl.

"Are you insane?" Josh said when Max told them the news.

"No, it's just something I have to do."

"We'll come with you," Bella said.

"We will?" Josh asked in a squeaky voice.

"Of course we will. Someone has to have Max's back in case Snarl tries to strangle him."

"Hey guys, I appreciate the thought, but this is something I have to do on my own. I'll see you later."

When Max arrived at the hospital, he didn't know Snarl's real name, so he wasn't sure how to find him.

"Hi, I'm looking for a boy about age fourteen or fifteen, who looks like a gorilla, and came in recently with two broken legs."

"Do you know his name?" the nurse behind the desk asked.

"Everyone at school calls him Snarl," Max said.

"I know exactly who you mean," the nurse said. "He's the rude boy in room twenty-three. You're his first visitor, and I'm sure you know why."

Max nodded, then headed off in the direction the nurse pointed and found Snarl with both his legs up in the air in traction.

"What are you doing here?" Snarl asked in his usual snarly voice.

"I just came to see how you're doing."

"Well, beat it!"

"The nurse told me you don't get any visitors. Don't you want one?"

Snarl stared at him. "It might be nice to have a visitor."

So Max told Snarl about Cyrus and how they had stopped the bank robbers together, and how Cyrus got the shoplifter caught in the mall.

"Visiting hours will be over in five minutes," said a voice over the intercom.

Max went home, but went back to the hospital to visit Snarl every day.

After Max had been visiting for almost two weeks, Snarl seemed friendlier.

"The Doc says I can go home tomorrow."

"Are you coming to school this week?"

"No, but at least I'll be out of here. I have to rest for a while at home, and then I can go back to school."

The next week, Snarl went back to school in a wheelchair. He was different. He actually shook hands, and patted other kids on the back, while Carl stood to the side looking confused.

When Snarl saw Max, he wheeled himself right over. "Max, it's good to see you, buddy! How did you know that visiting me in the hospital was exactly what I needed? It made me think about things differently. You know, you are the only one who visited me, despite the fact that I kept trying to take your lunch money!"

"Uh, you're not going to believe this, Snarl, but I read a verse in the Bible that says, 'Love your enemies.' I just knew the moment I read it that I needed to visit you in the hospital."

"A verse? I never would have guessed." Snarl held his hand out. "Thank you, Max."

Max shook his hand. Despite fearing his hand was about to be crushed, it was a very gentle handshake.

"Well, Max, I have to get to class. See you later?"

"Uh, okay," Max said.

"By the way, my name is Ashley, not Snarl— from now on, okay?"

"Uh, sure...Snar...Ashley."

Ashley smiled broadly, then turned and wheeled himself off to class.

CHAPTER 17

A WEEK LATER, MAX CELEBRATED HIS TWELFTH birthday. He invited Bella, Josh, and of course Mindy as well. Cyrus, Tara, and Max's parents were all there to give him gifts and make his birthday special.

When the cake came out with twelve candles, everyone sang Happy Birthday. They all sang loudly and happily, except for Cyrus who couldn't sing. Then Max got presents from everyone. He got a soft leather baseball glove that fit his hand perfectly. He also got the Bug Zapper 2 game and a check from his grandma.

"This is the best birthday ever!" Max said at the end of his party.

A few days later, Max went shopping with the money from his grandma and the money he had been given when Cyrus stopped the shoplifter. He finally had enough to buy a brand new skateboard. He chose a black one with cool flames on top and a snake with huge fangs painted on the bottom.

Max rode the skateboard home. He was a bit shaky at first, but he was a fast learner. Soon he was coasting along, pushing off with his foot whenever he needed a burst of speed.

When Max got back home, he burst into the house, so excited to show off his new skateboard. "Look Mom! Look at my new skateboard! Isn't it great?"

"That's nice, Max, but have you written to thank your grandma for the money she sent?"

"Not yet..."

"Well, now would be a good time. Now you can tell her what you bought with it. I'm sure she'd love to hear about that."

"Okay, Mom." Max headed off to his room.

When he had finished the letter, he was about to head downstairs when he noticed Cyrus bouncing against the bars of his cage. "Do you want to come with me, Cyrus?"

Cyrus jumped up and down.

"Okay, buddy." Max took Cyrus out of the cage.

"Do you have a stamp, Mom?" Max asked once he got downstairs.

"No, you'll have to get one at the post office. Are you going to mail that right now?"

"Can I? Then I can ride my skateboard!"

"Sure, go ahead."

So Max took his letter and zipped down to the post office on his skateboard, with Cyrus poking his little head out of the shirt pocket enjoying the wind on his face. When Max arrived there was a long line of people. He got in line and waited while it moved forward slowly.

A couple minutes later, a man with a shotgun burst into the post office. "Where's Mr. Griffin?" he roared. "I've got something for him!"

The women behind the counter looked scared, but one of them said to the man with the shotgun, "Now Curly, you don't want to hurt anyone. Can't we talk about this? Shooting Mr. Griffin isn't going to make up for him firing you."

"Maybe not, but I'll sure feel better!" Curly hollered. "Now go get Mr. Griffin!"

Meanwhile, Cyrus was trying to get out of Max's shirt pocket, so Max took him out and set him on the floor.

One of the women went into a back room and a few moments later came back with a short, balding man.

Curly grabbed Mr. Griffin, pulling him out from behind the counter and shoving him into the open. Then he leveled the gun at him.

"Please don't hurt me!" Mr. Griffin sobbed.

"You should have thought about that before you fired me!"

"But what else could I have done? You were late almost every day, and weren't getting all your work done. I needed someone I could depend on."

"That makes no difference, I'm still gonna give you what you deserve!" Curly said as he aimed the shotgun at Mr. Griffin.

What Curly hadn't noticed was that Cyrus had been busy. He had managed to sneak up to Curly and was slowly climbing up the back of his pant leg. When he got to Curly's untucked shirt, he slipped inside. Suddenly Curly let out a shriek and grabbed for his back, just as Cyrus slipped away, ran down his pant leg and across the floor back to Max. Most everyone saw Cyrus then, except for Curly.

Curly lifted his shirt, trying to feel what had hurt so much.

Max could see a group of red spots. It looked like Cyrus had stabbed Curly with his quills.

As Curly felt around on his back and sobbed from the pain, the shotgun slipped out of his hand, fell to the floor and went off, blasting a hole in the ceiling.

A couple men who had been in line to get stamps grabbed Curly. One of the women behind the counter had enough presence of mind to grab a roll of wide packing tape and toss it to one of the men. Then the men taped Curly's arms to his sides by winding the tape around him a few times. They did the same to his feet, and before long Curly was on the floor completely helpless.

Nobody got their letters mailed or stamps bought until after the police came and took Curly away. Afterwards everyone wanted to come up and shake Max's hand and Cyrus' little paw. Cyrus grinned while everyone shook his paw.

It seemed Max and Cyrus had a talent for stopping bad guys.

ABOUT THE AUTHOR

AT THE AGE OF FIVE, WHEN MOST CHILDREN ARE PLAYING outside with friends, Dave Hammer was lying in a hospital bed, recovering from burns inflicted in a tragic accident. His creativity helped him to learn to do everything despite the odds against him. Now he uses his creativity to write books. His first book, *From Out of the Flames: A True Story of Survival* tells the account about his life. His second book, *Wacked: Hey Wanna Squeeze My Cheese?* is a book filled with funny poems showcasing his special brand of humor. Dave is an avid reader and lives in Western Canada where he writes full time.

To learn more about Dave Hammer's books, visit www.booksbydave.com.

Stay tuned for the next Max Greebly adventure!

When Max goes on a vacation with his family, he's expecting fun and relaxation–but when a pack of pick pockets start causing trouble for hotel guests, Max is in for another big adventure!